P9-DDB-055

THIS BOOK BELONGS TO:

____

A CAT
NAMED TIM

AND OTHER STORIES

FOR PAIGE, MOLLY, TYLER, AND ELEANOR

Thank-you: Anne Koyama, Ed Kanerva, Ryan North, Aaron Costain,
Jen Breach, Matt Forsythe, Mom, Dad, and especially Lindsay Archibald

Published by Koyama Press
koyamapress.com

First edition: September 2014

ISBN: 978-1-927668-10-8

Printed in China

Koyama Press gratefully acknowledges the Canada Council for the Arts
for their support of our publishing program.

A CAT NAMED TIM

AND OTHER STORIES

by John Martz

koyama press

DOUG & MOUSE

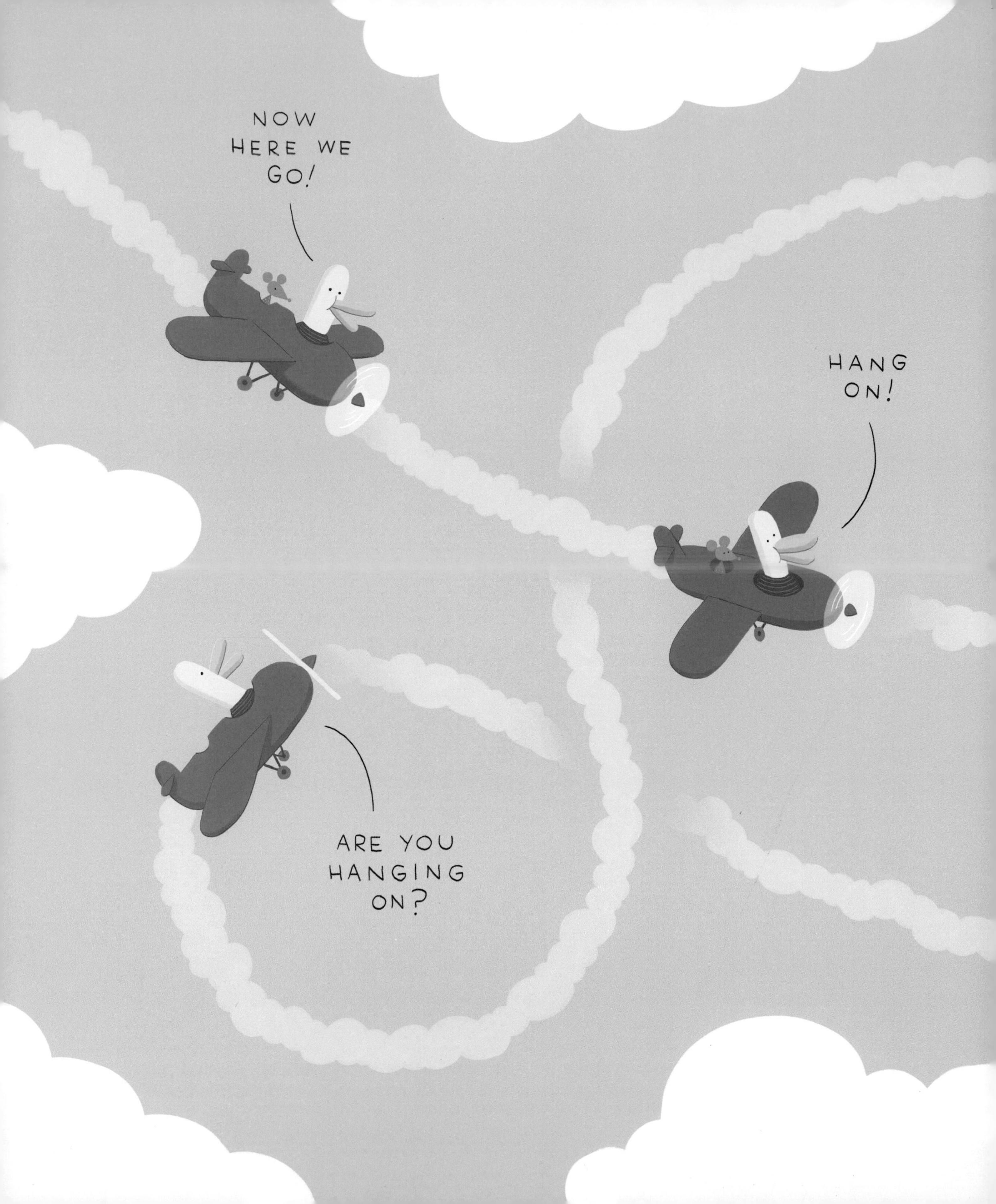
NOW HERE WE GO!
HANG ON!
ARE YOU HANGING ON?

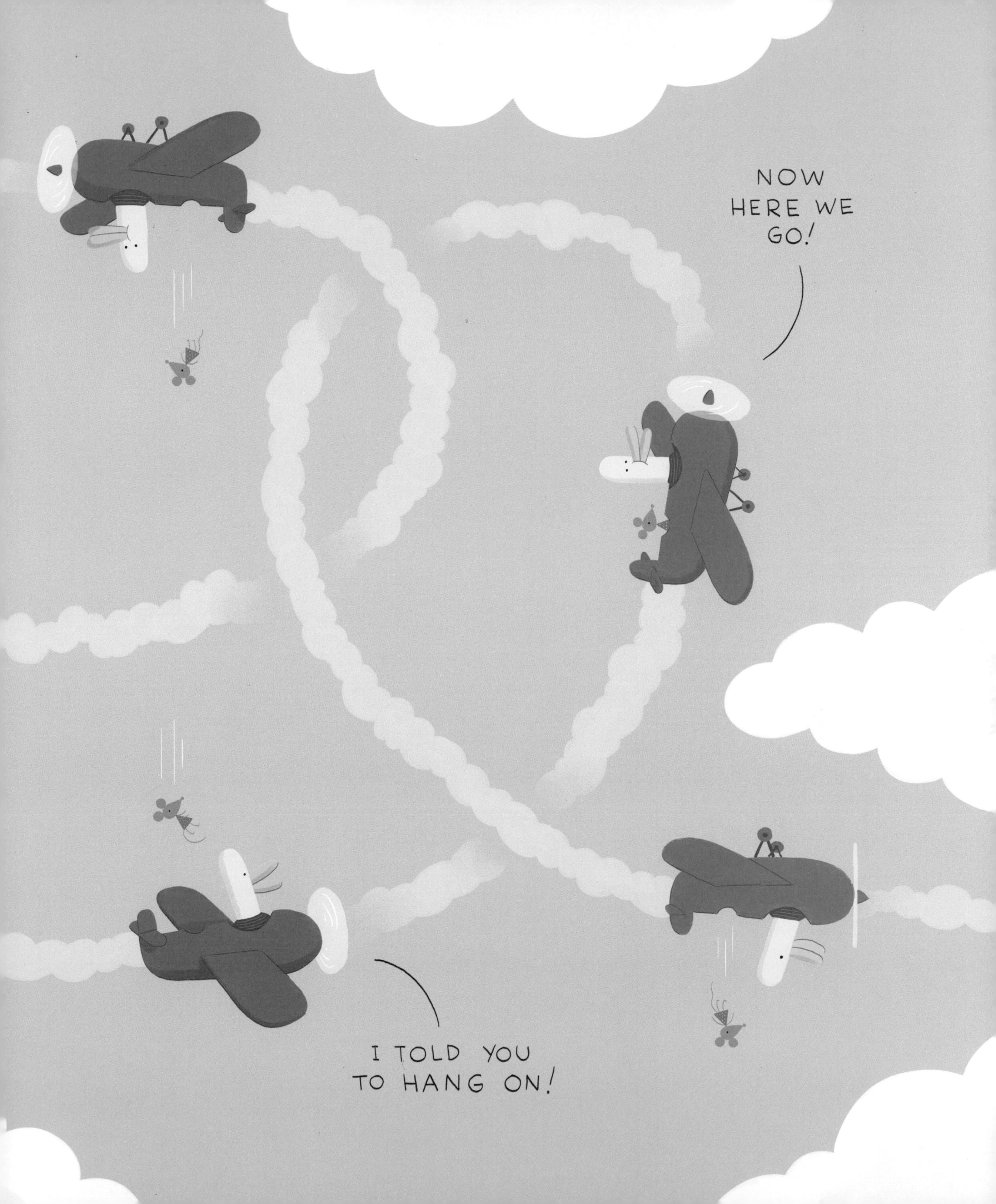
NOW HERE WE GO!
I TOLD YOU TO HANG ON!

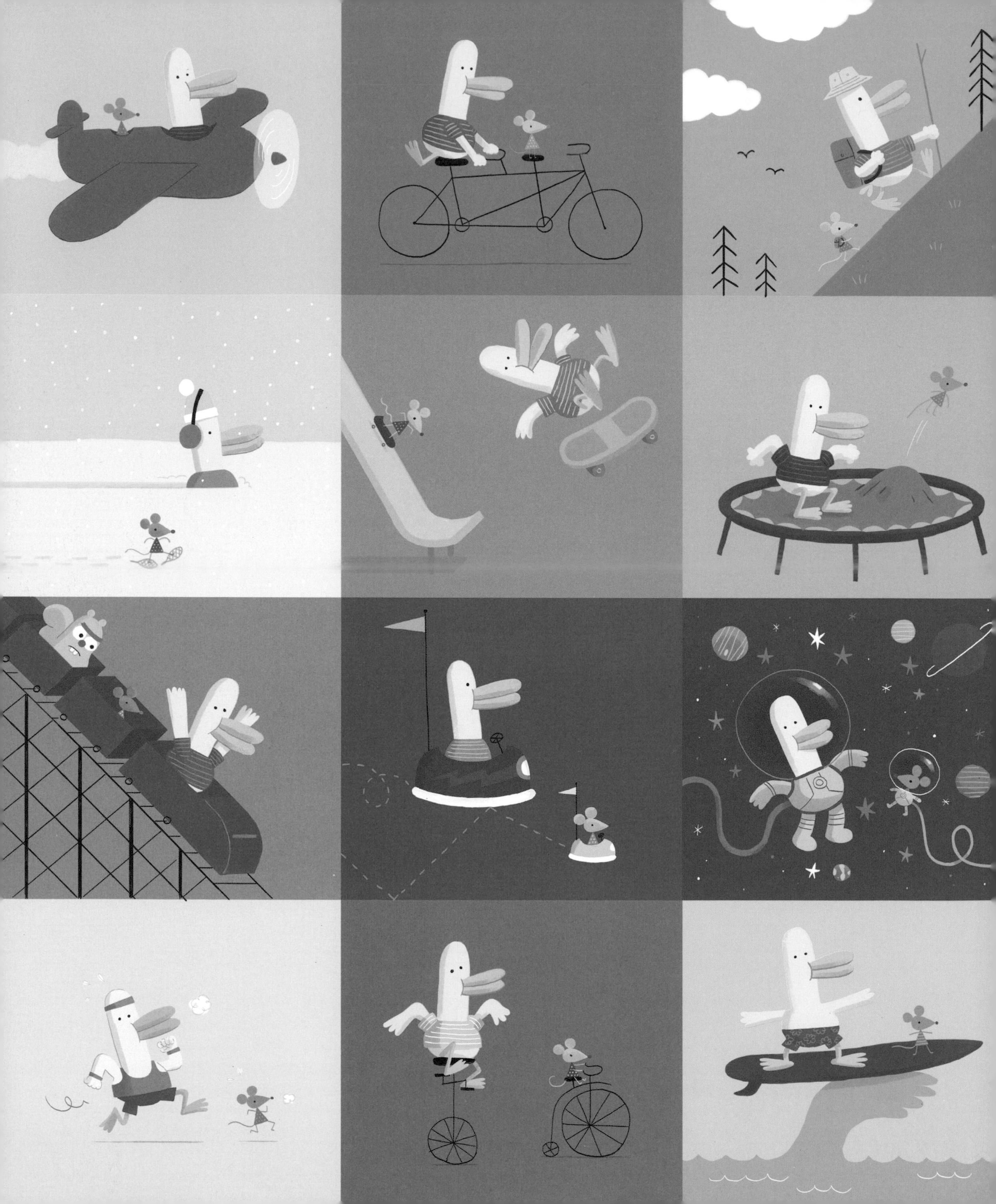

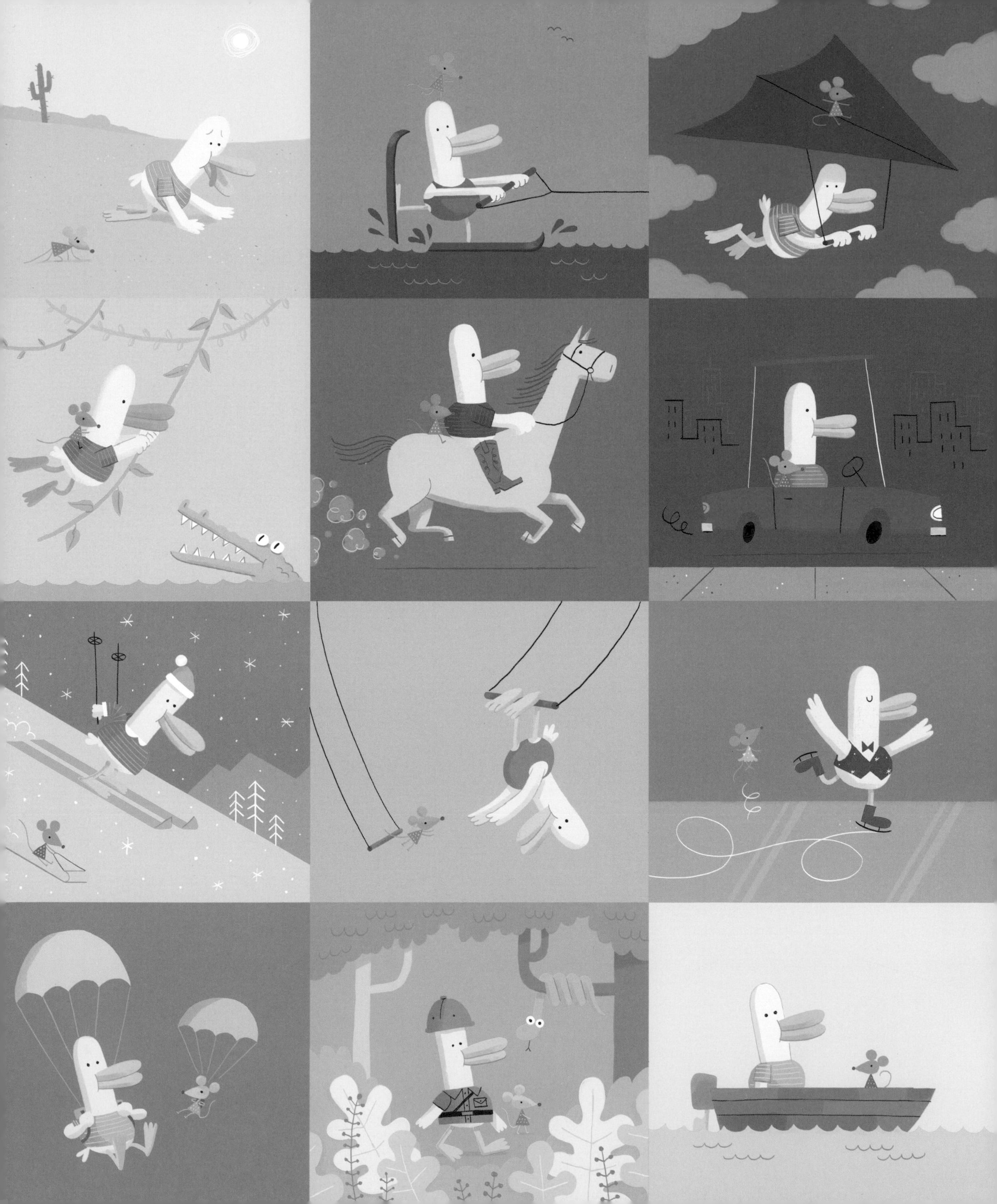

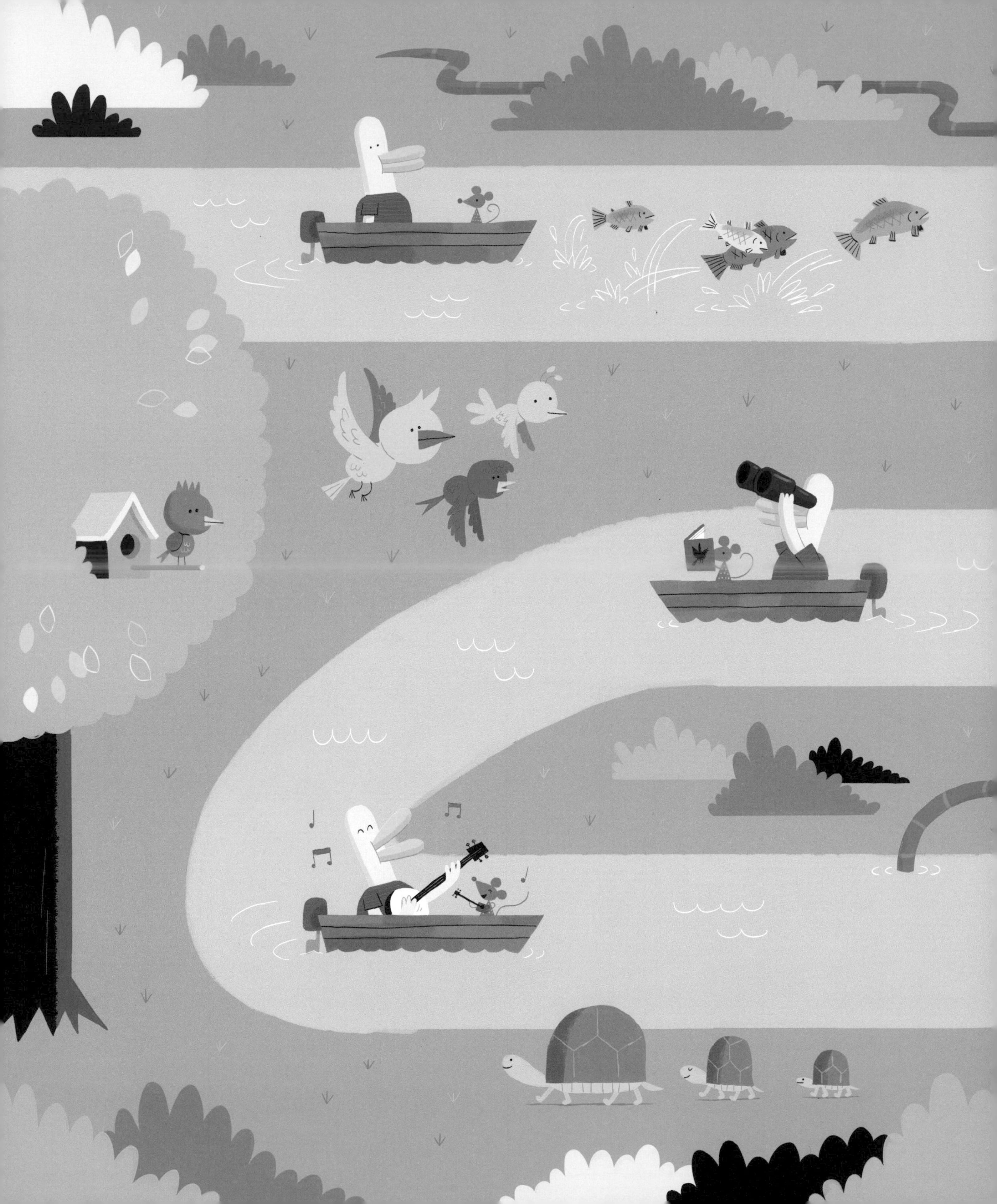

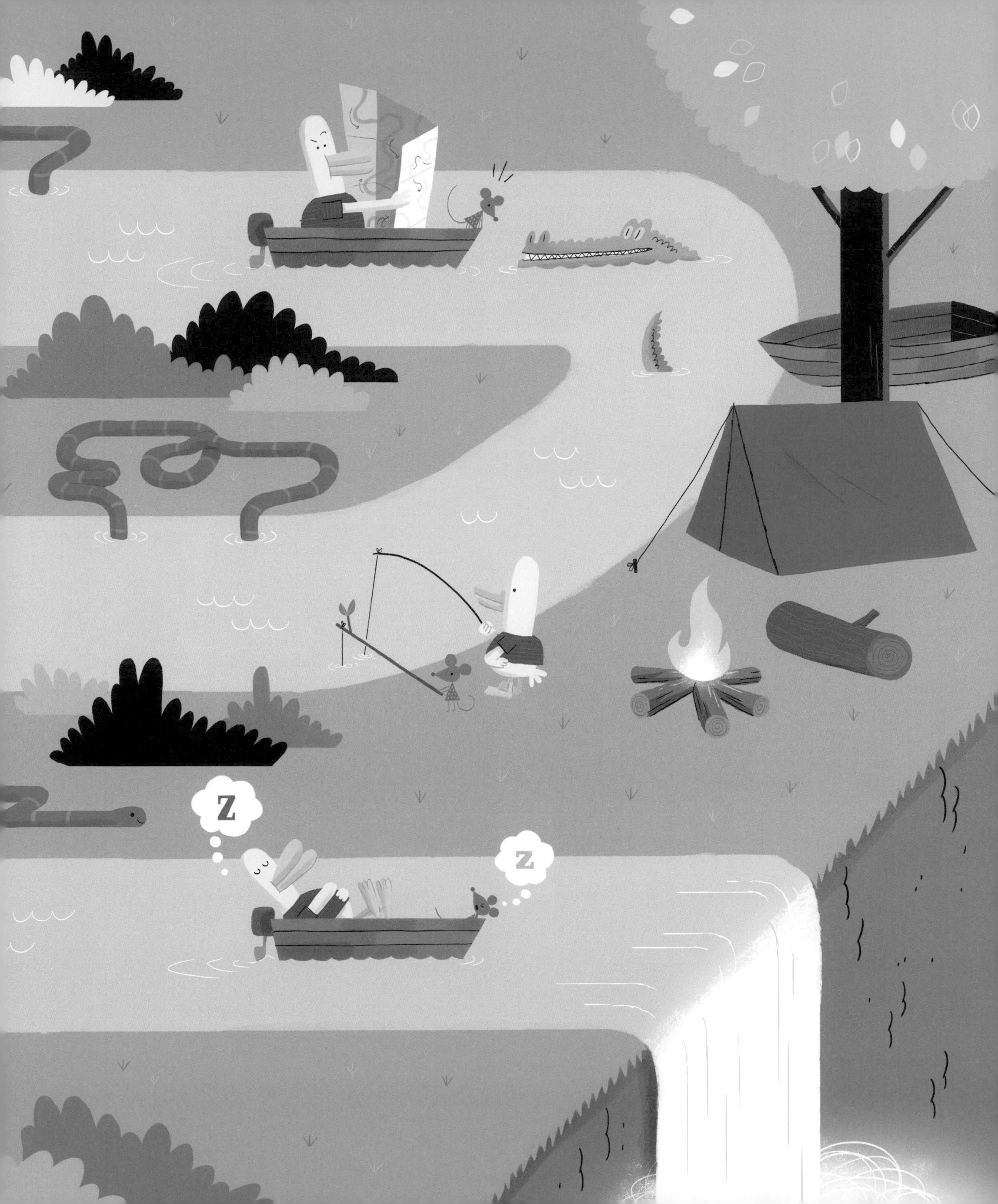
Z
Z

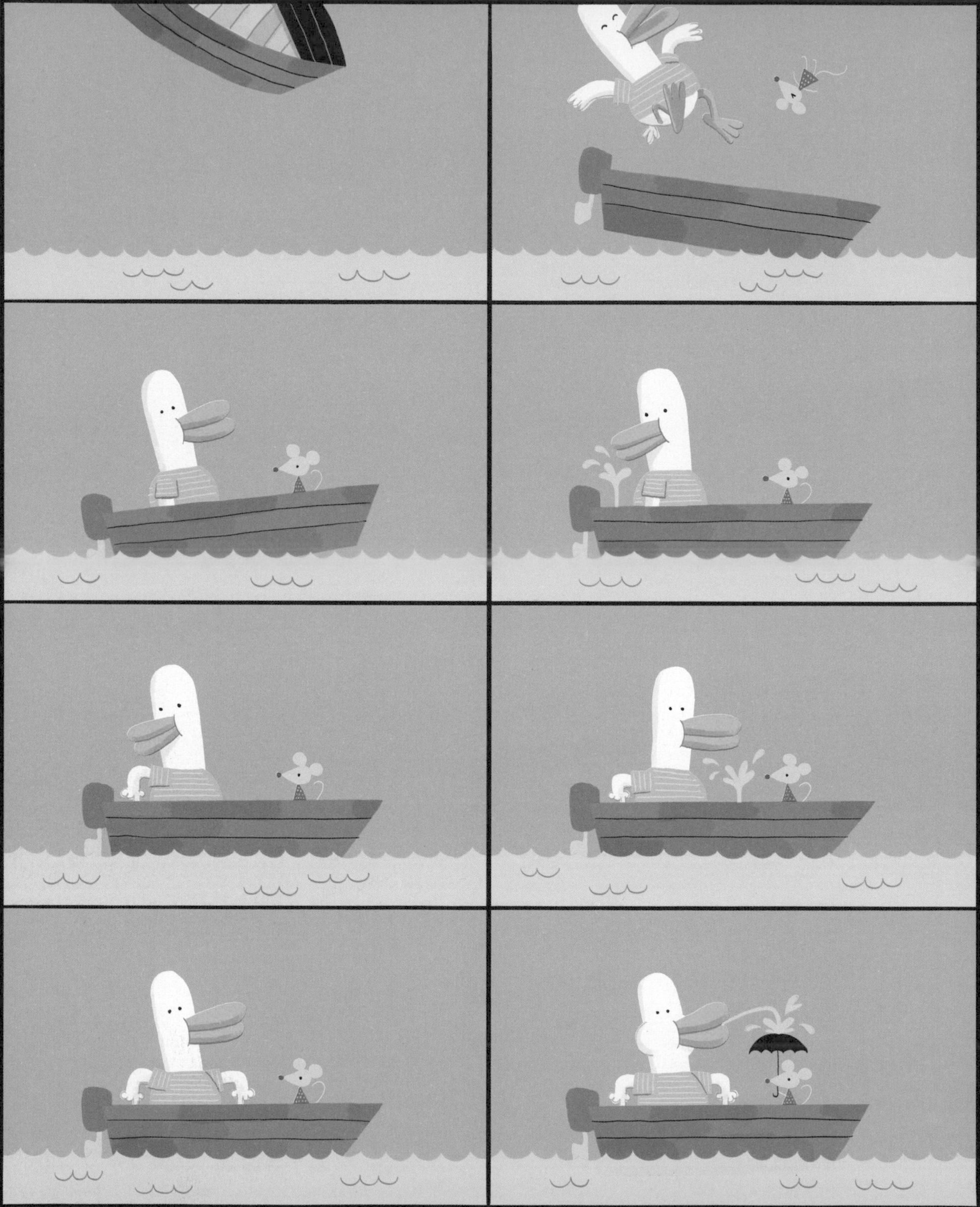

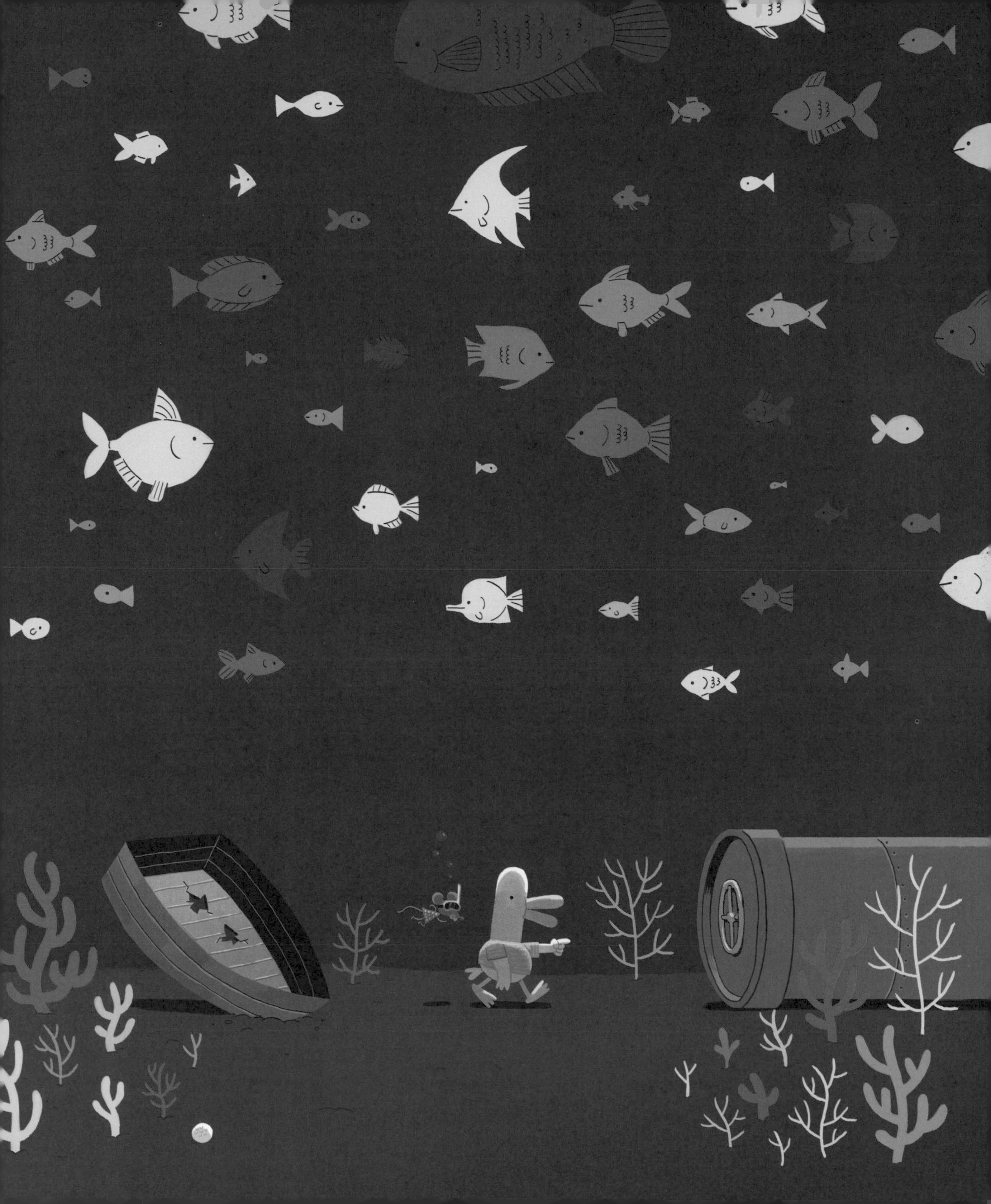

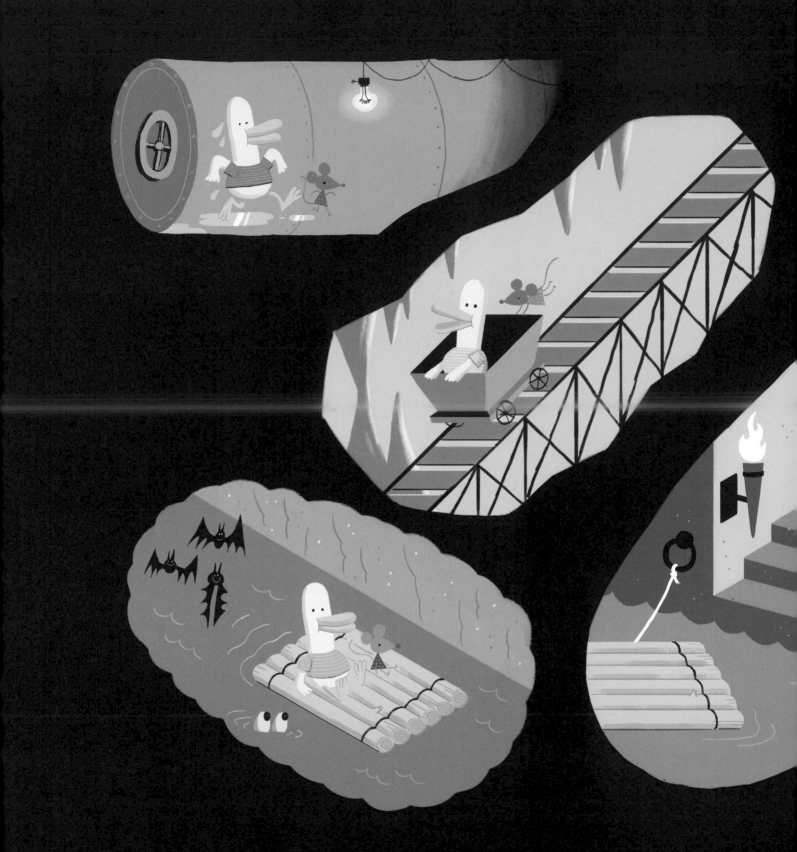

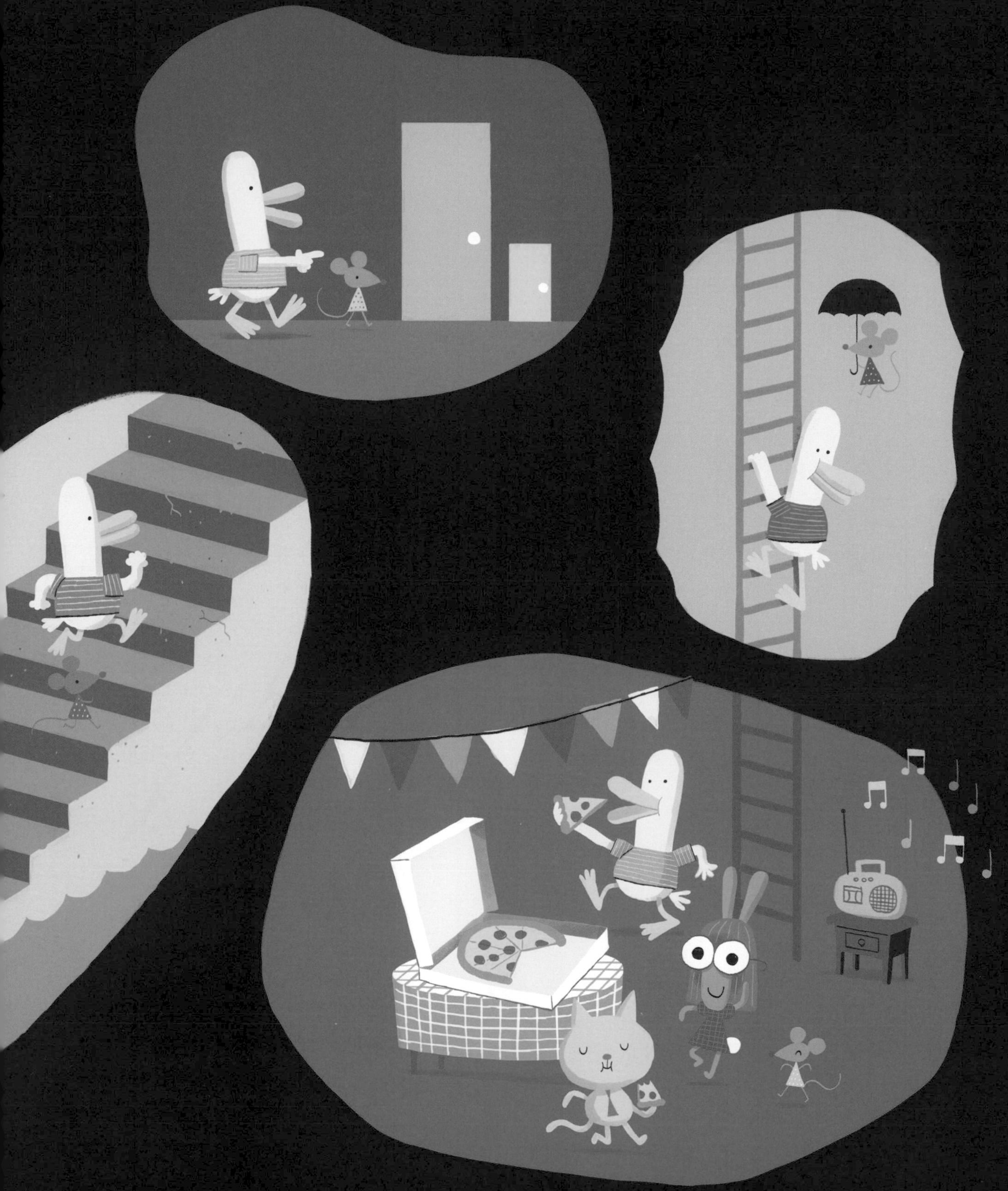

TIM

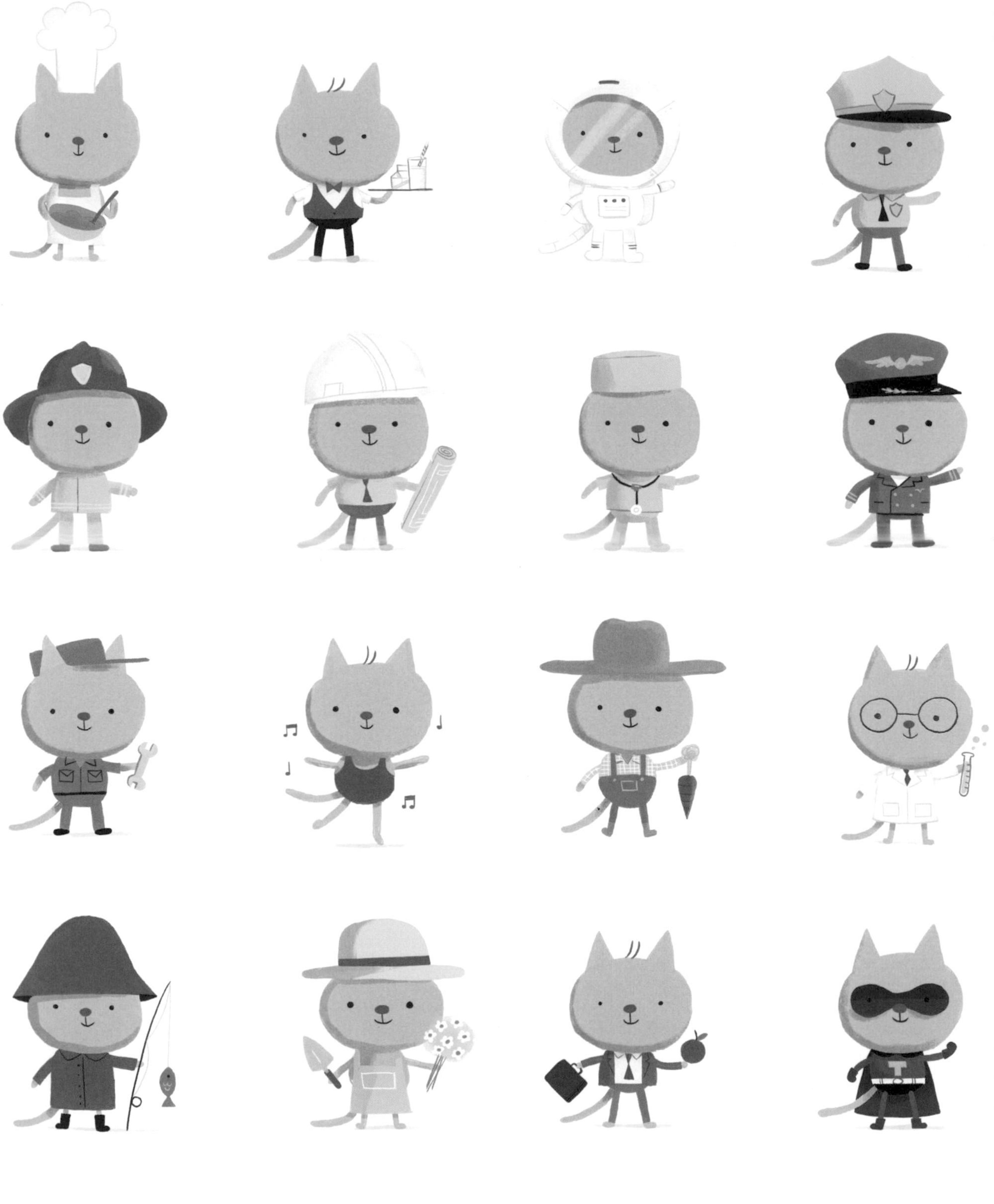

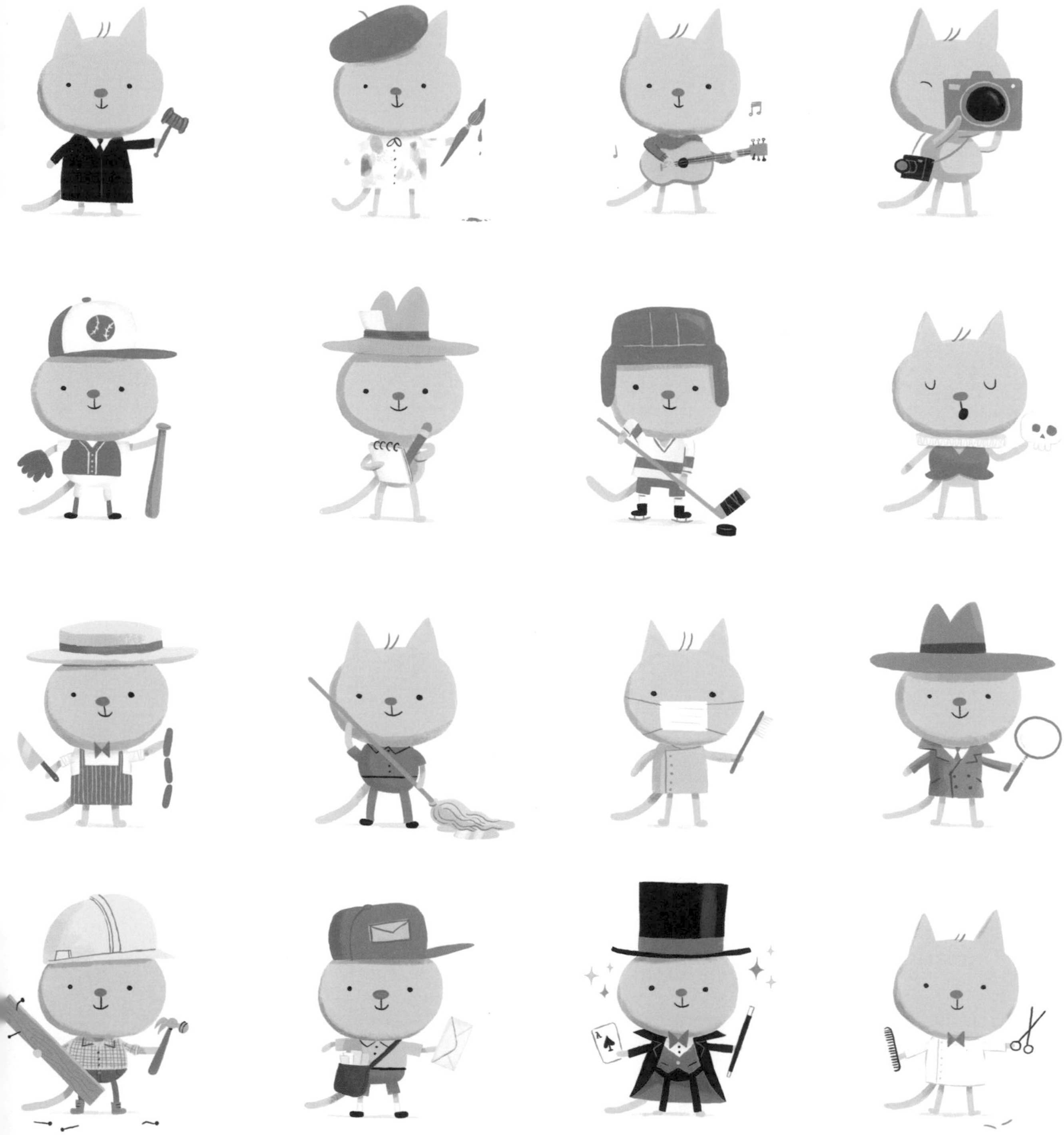

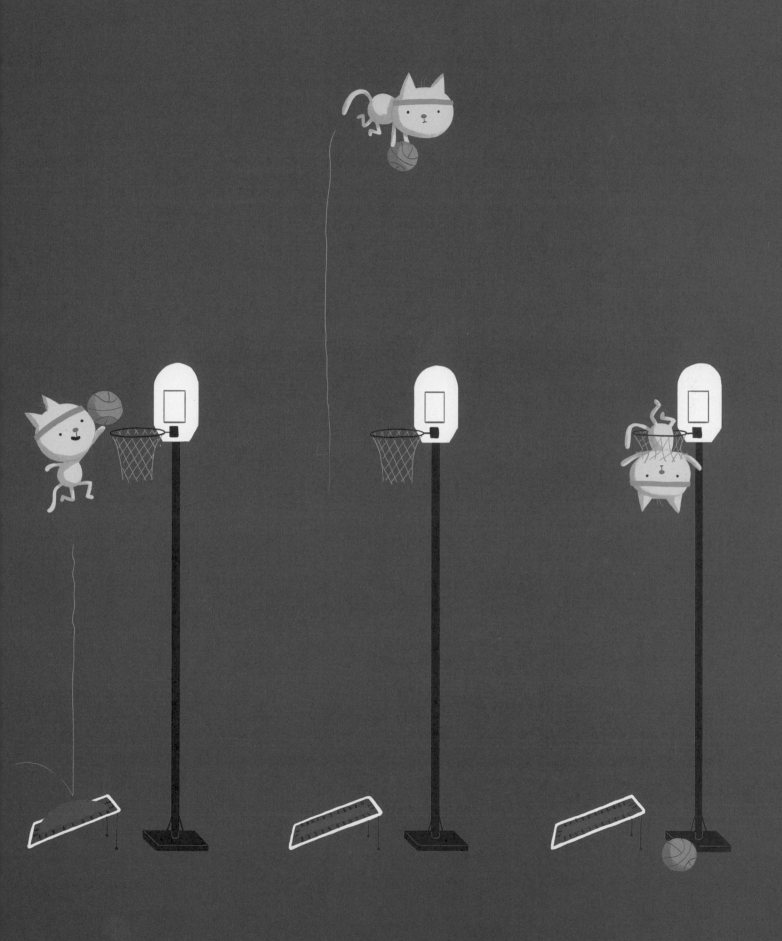

POOF
ZOP!
FFFT!

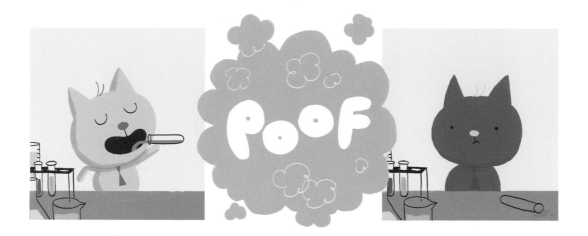

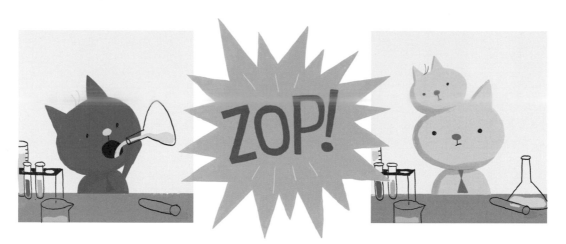

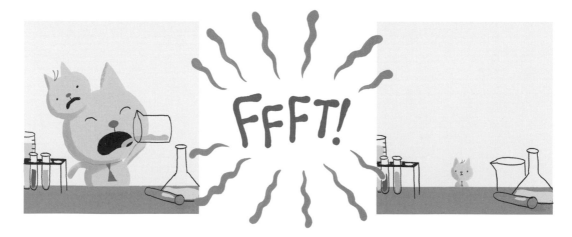

GLORP
BUNK!
tink!

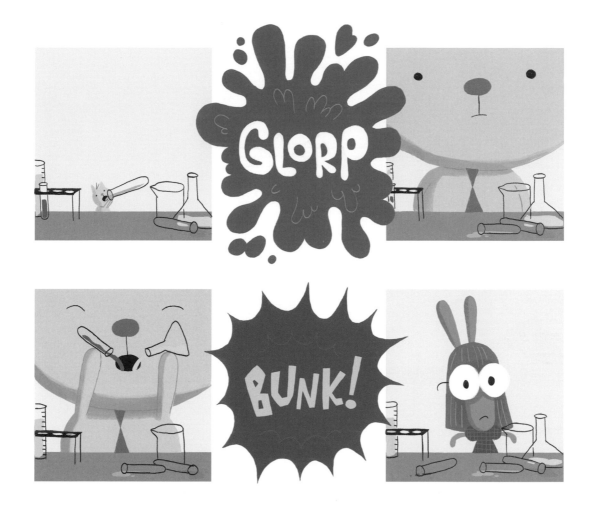

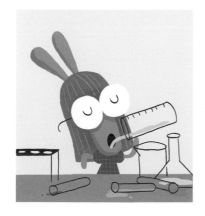

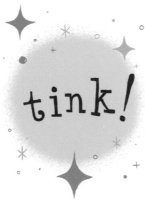

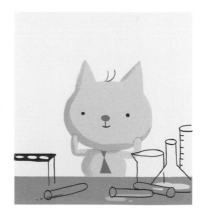

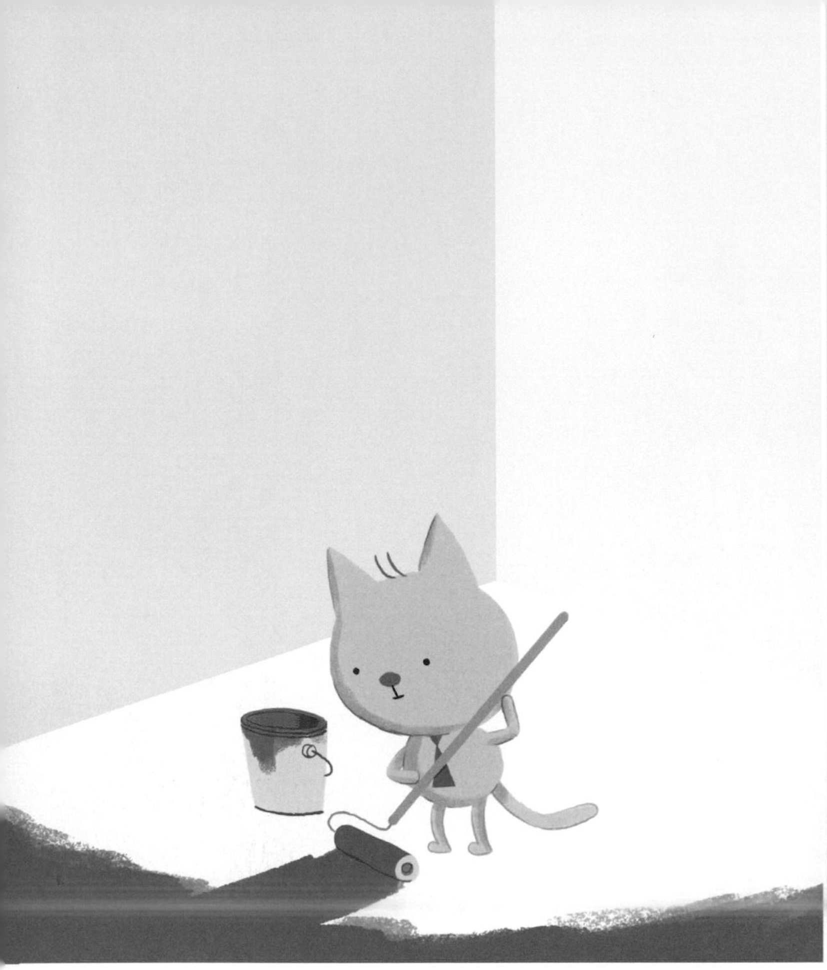
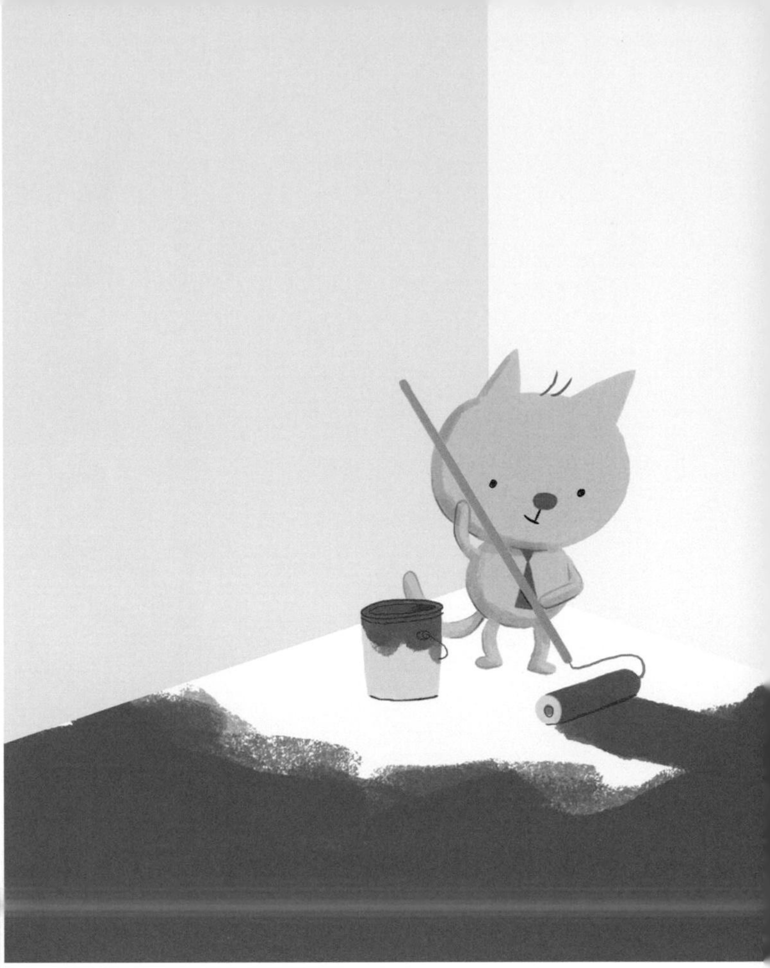
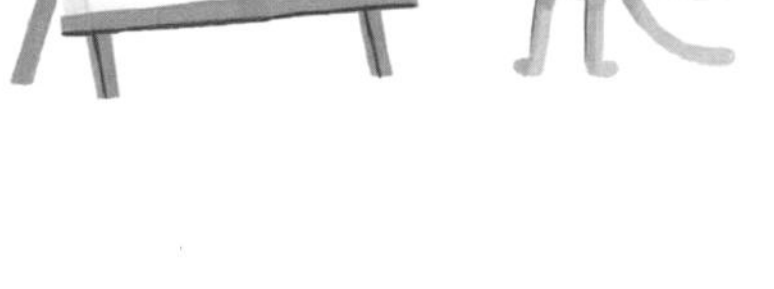
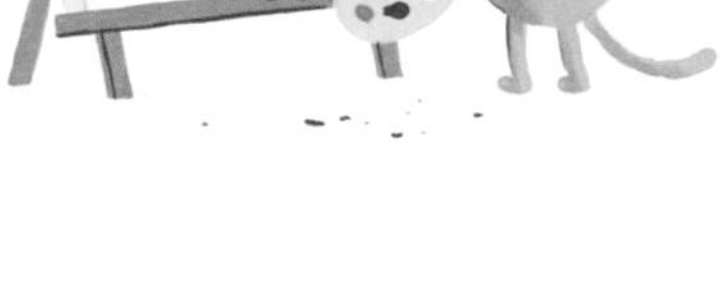
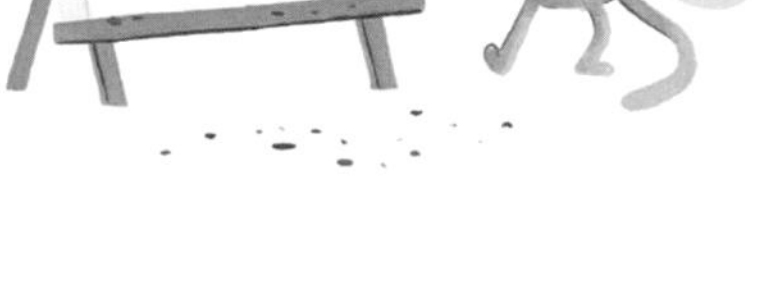

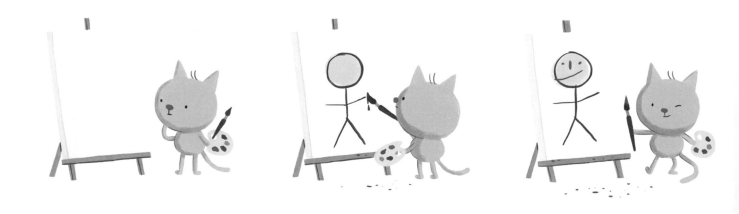

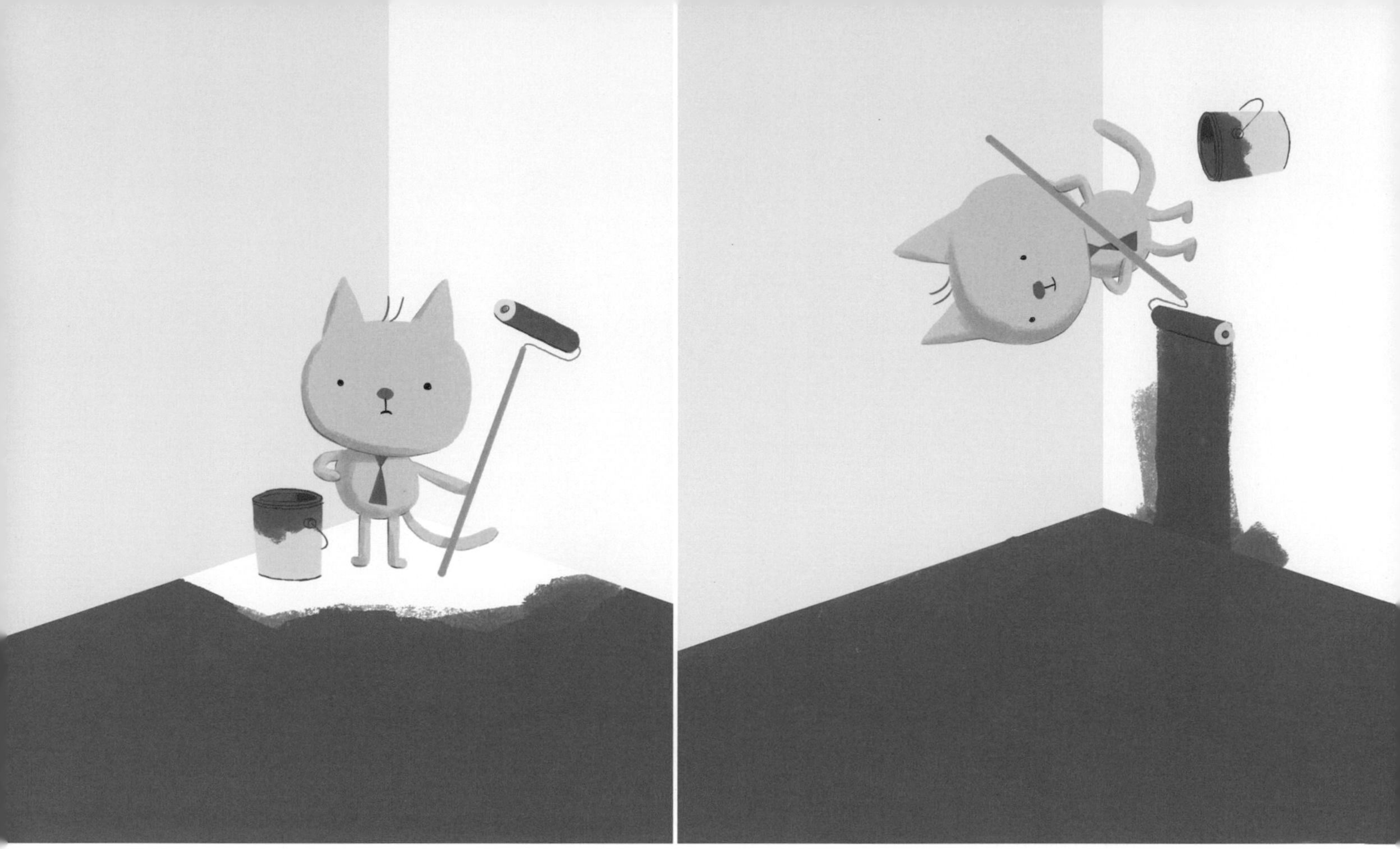

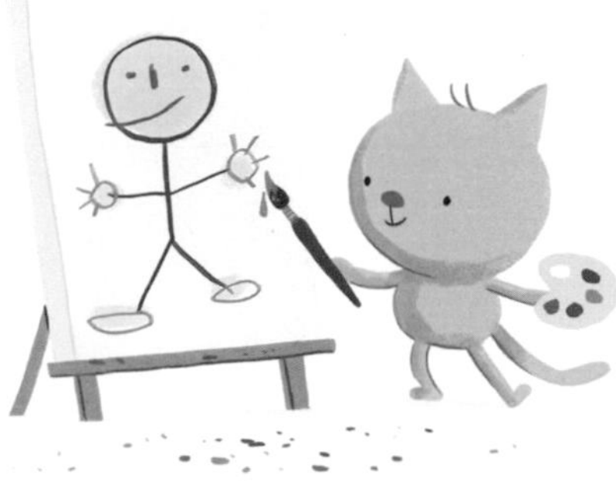

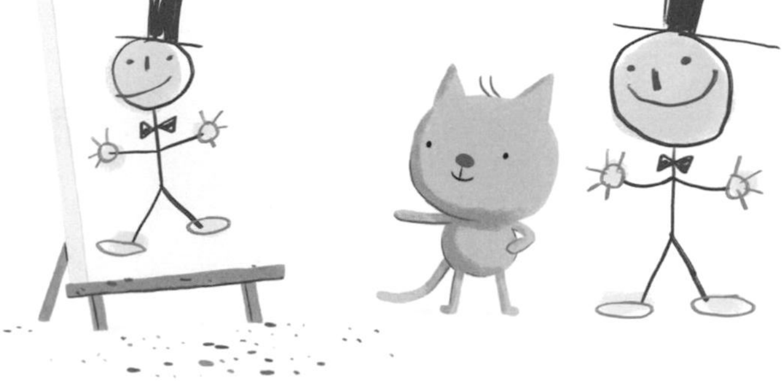

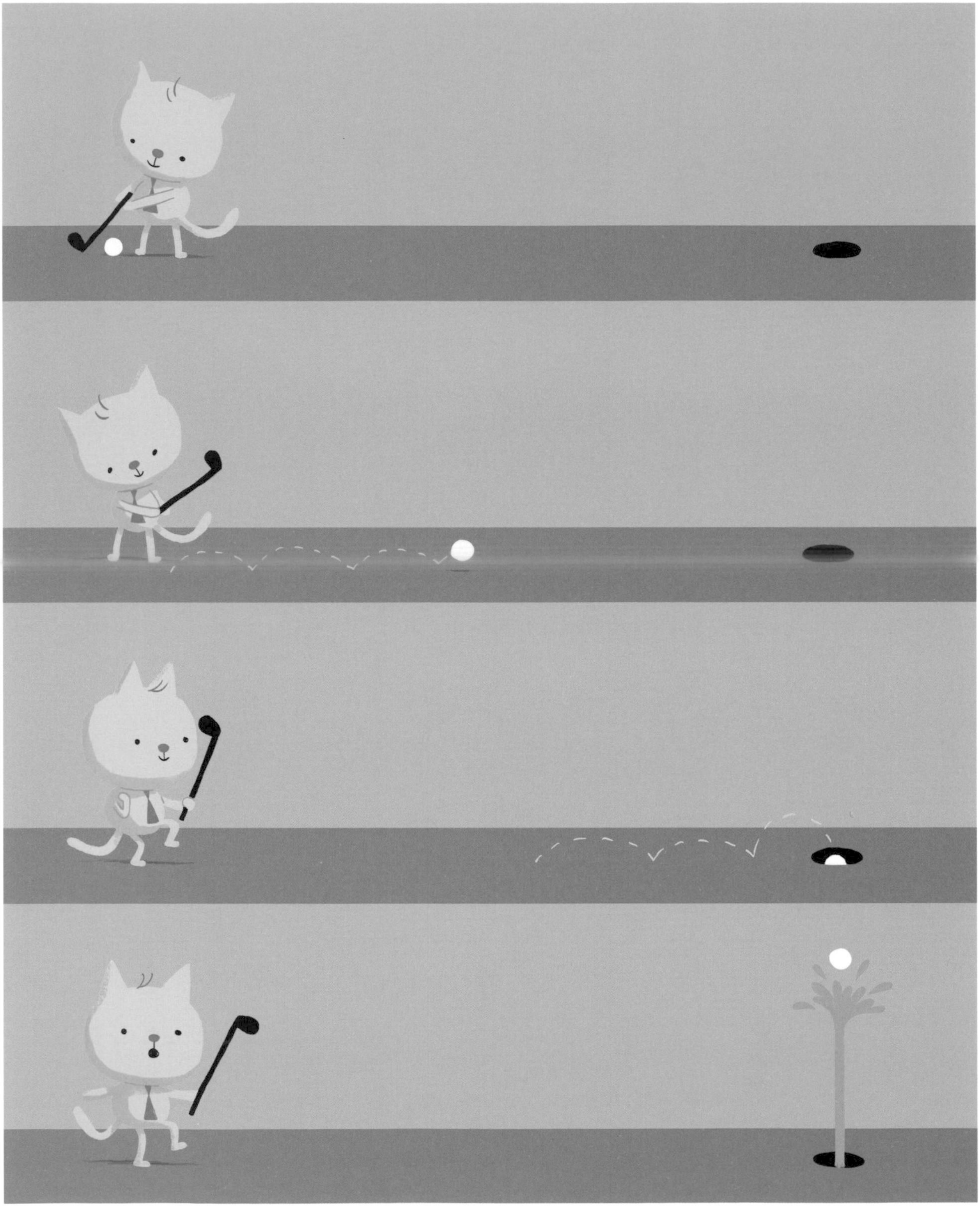

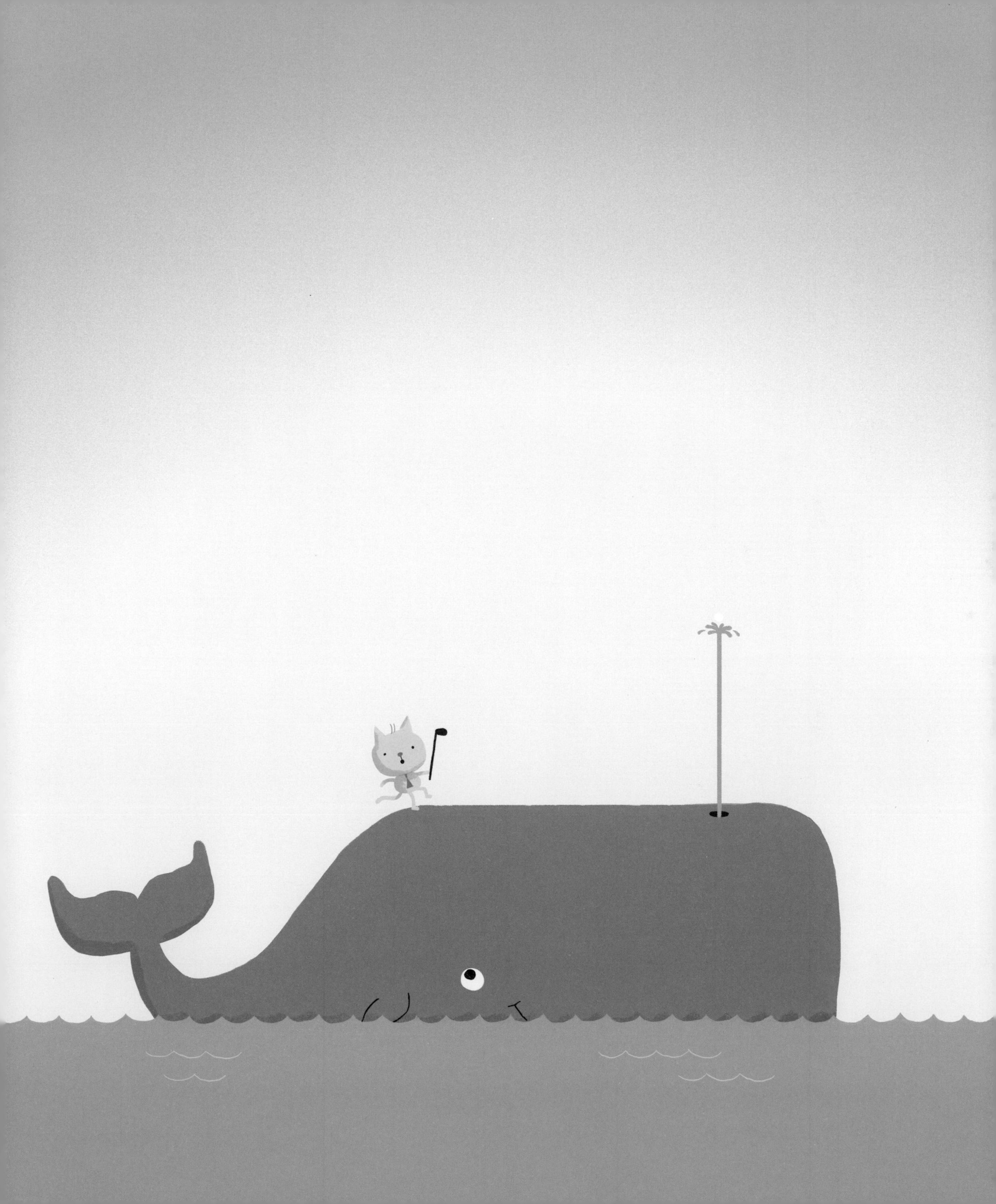

CONNIE

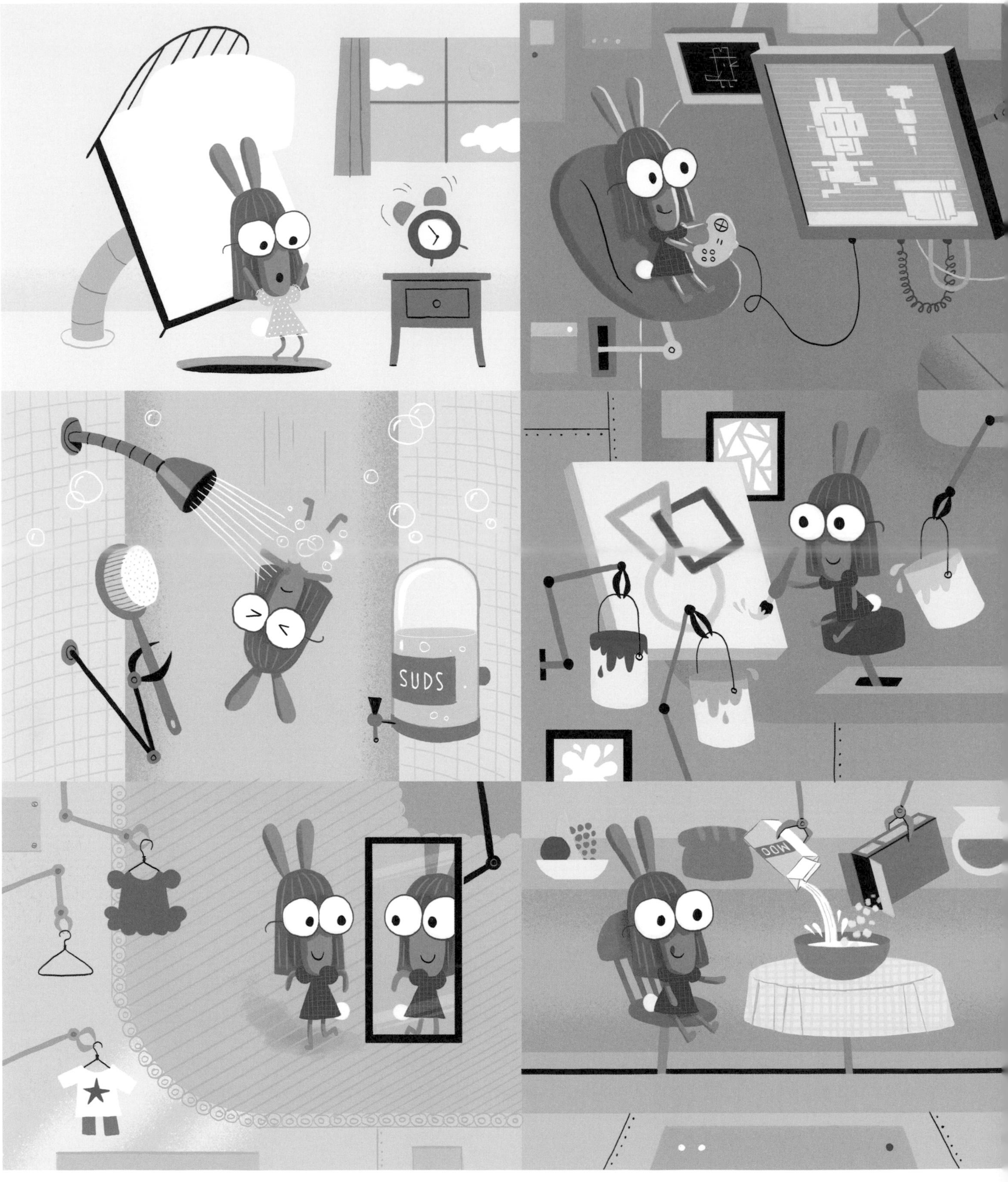
SUDS

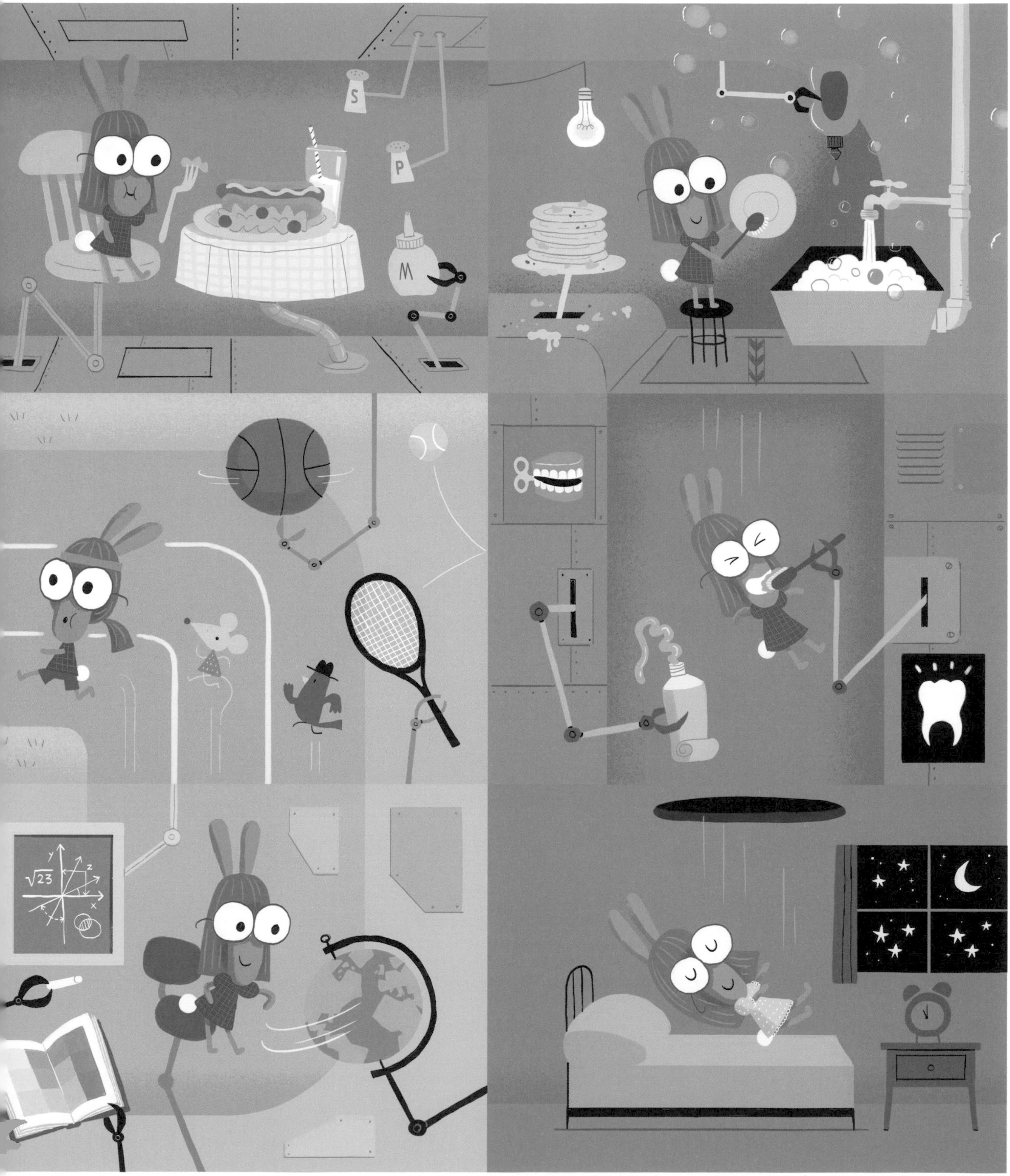
S
P
M
√23

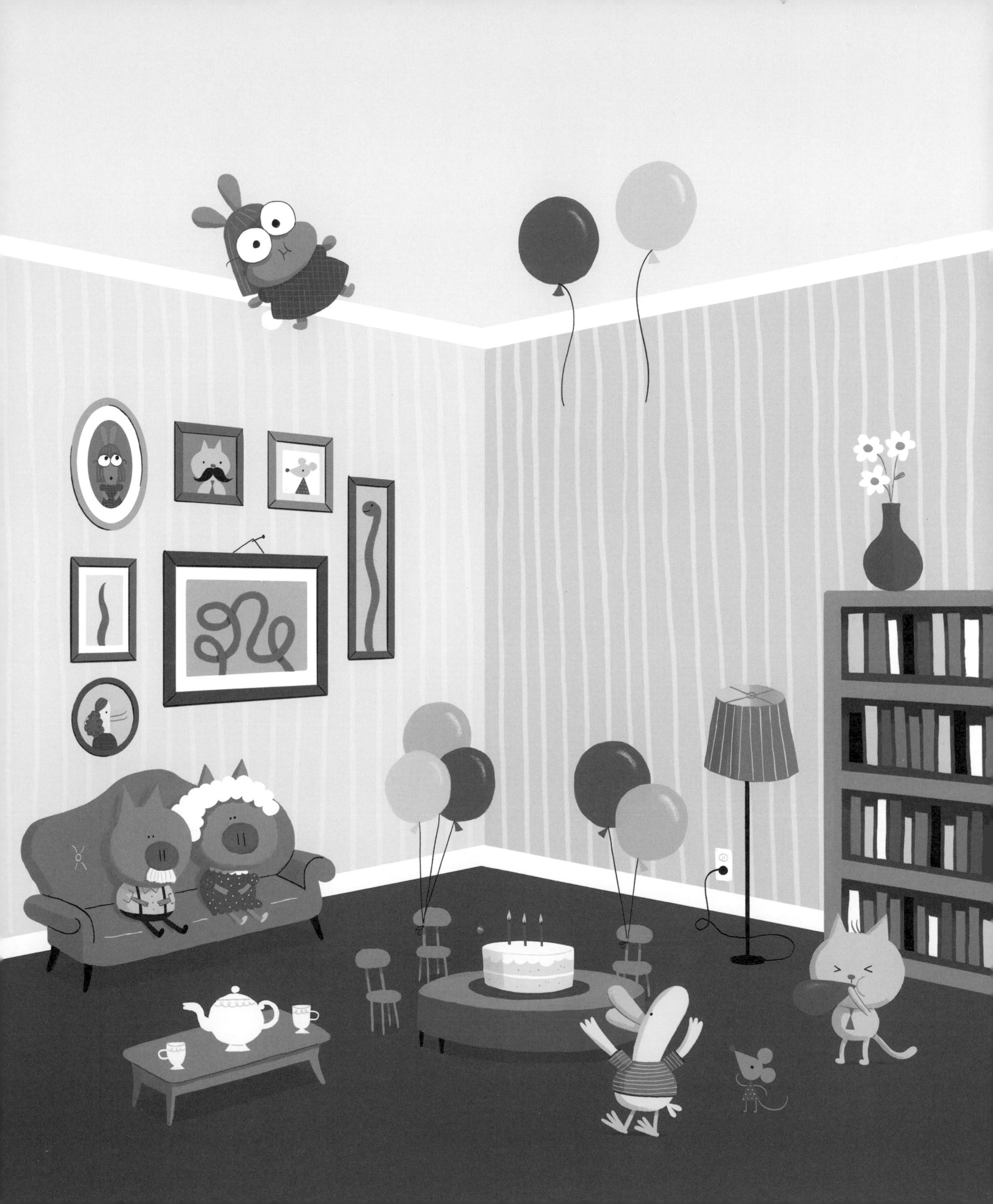

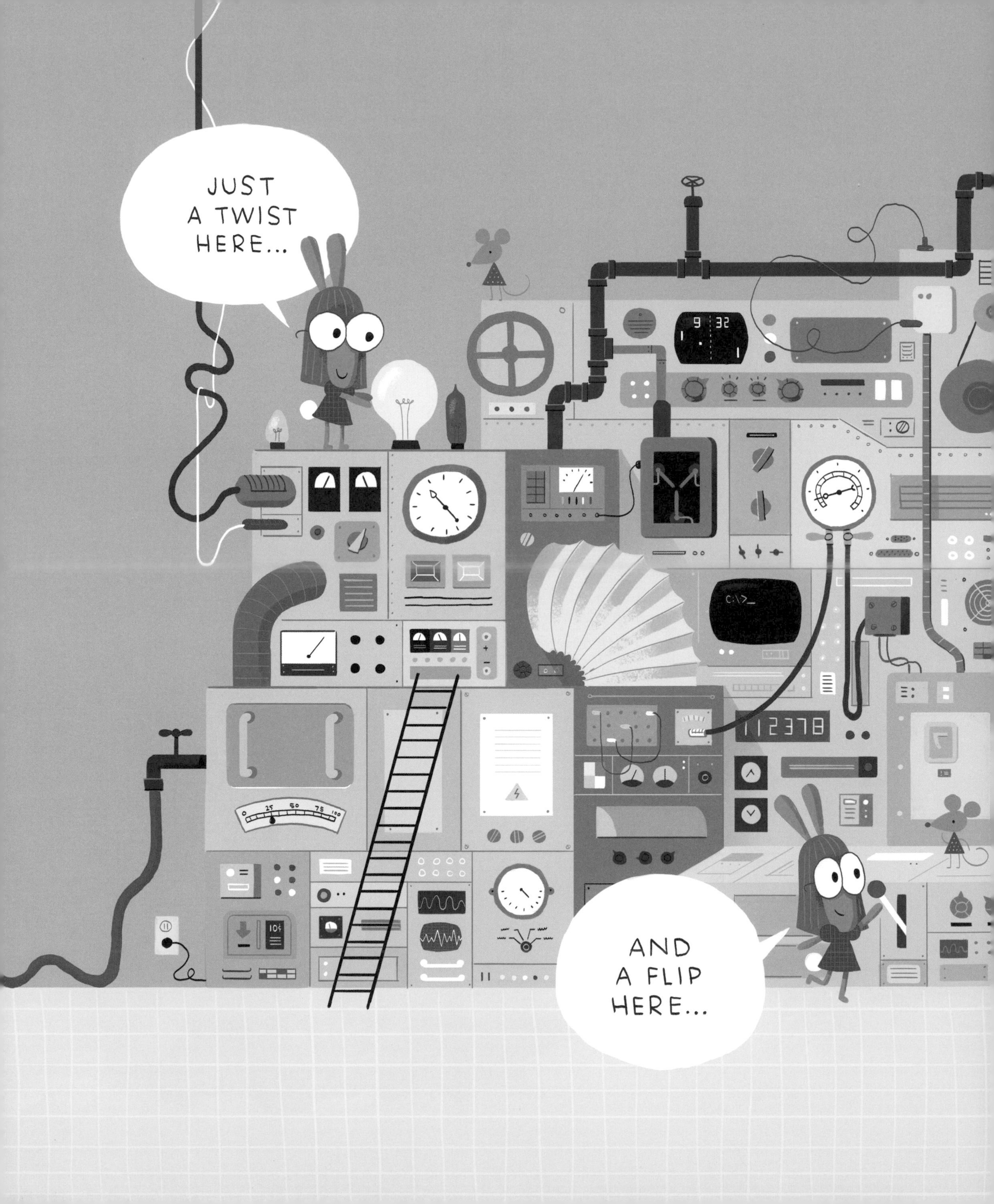
JUST A TWIST HERE...
AND A FLIP HERE...

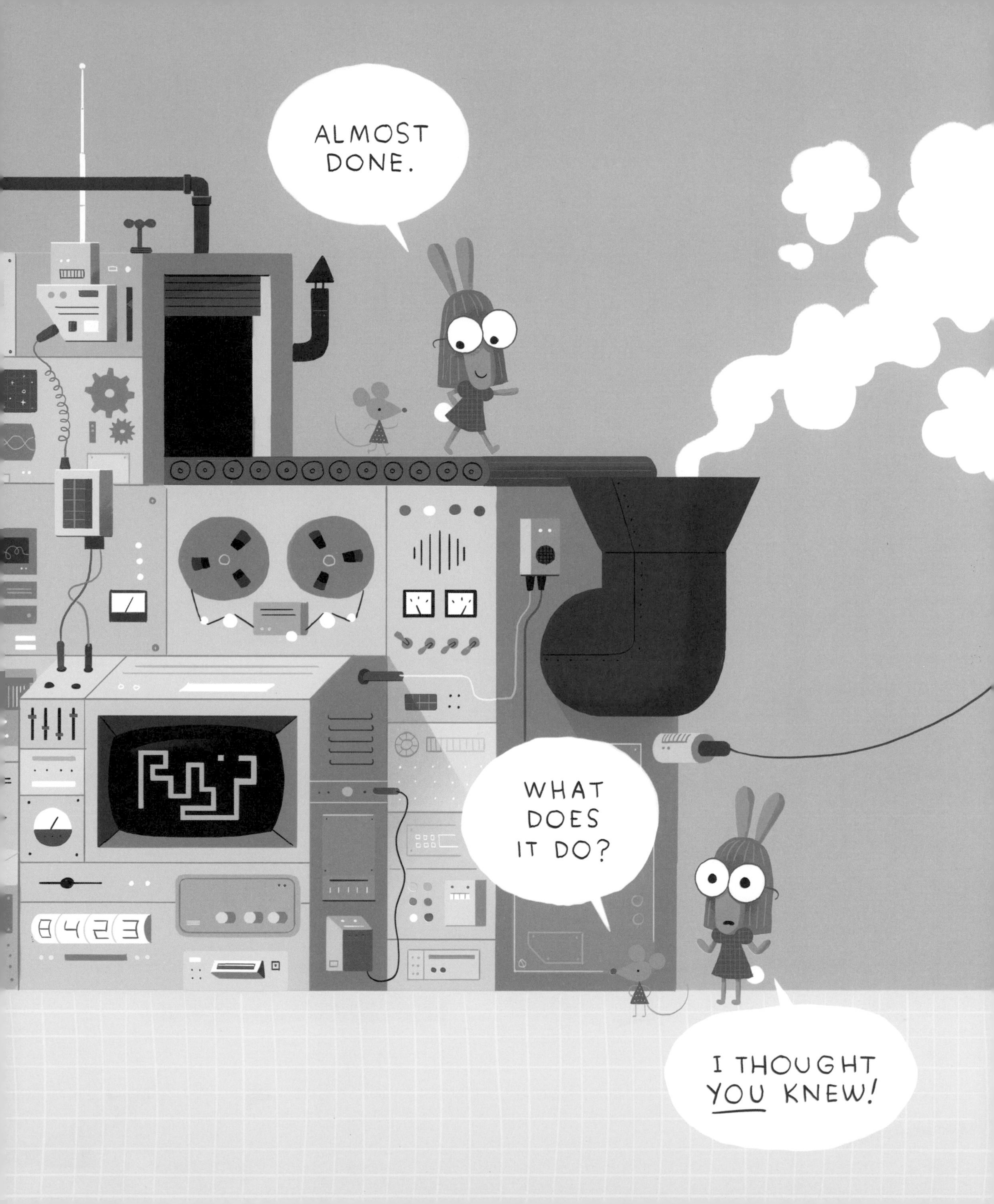
ALMOST DONE.
WHAT DOES IT DO?
I THOUGHT YOU KNEW!
8423

OPEN

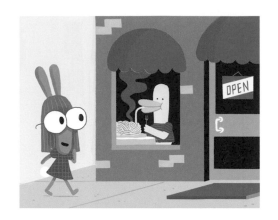

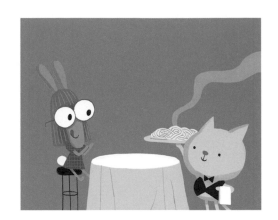

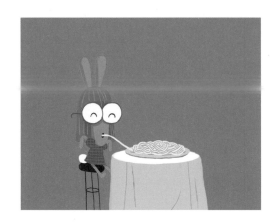

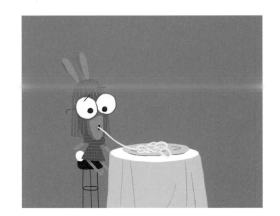

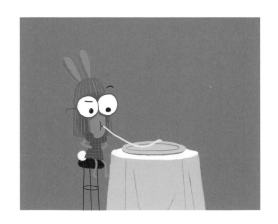

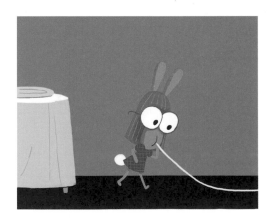

EXIT

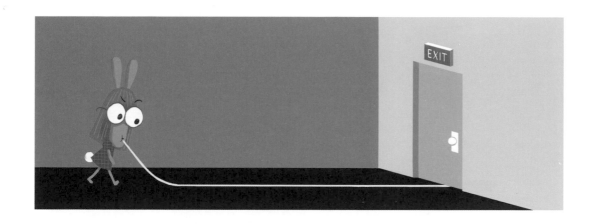

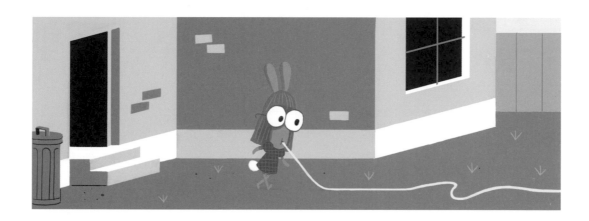

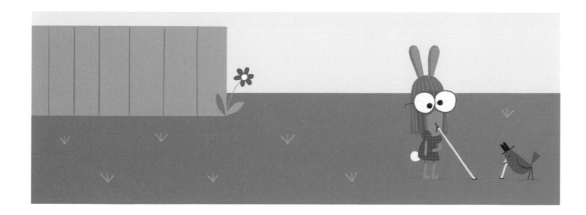

MR. & MRS. HAMHOCK

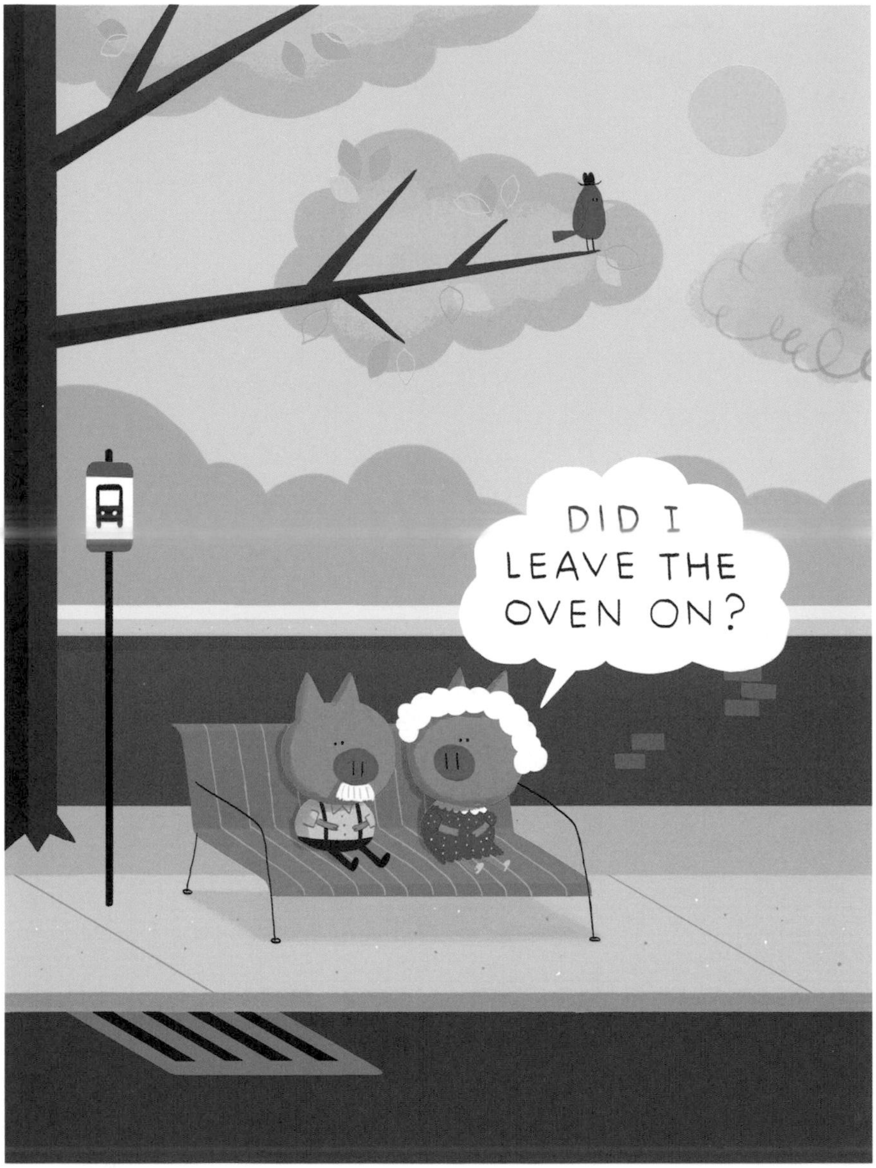
DID I LEAVE THE OVEN ON?

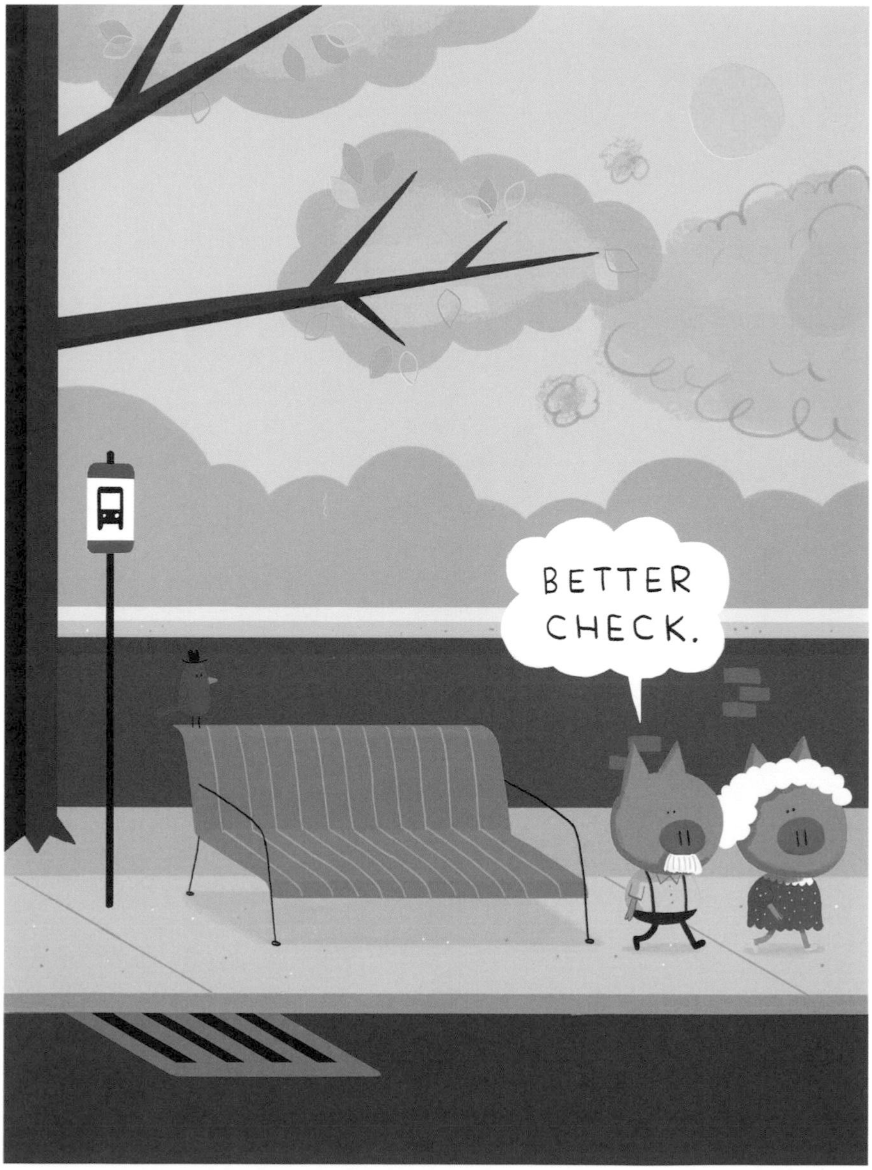
BETTER CHECK.

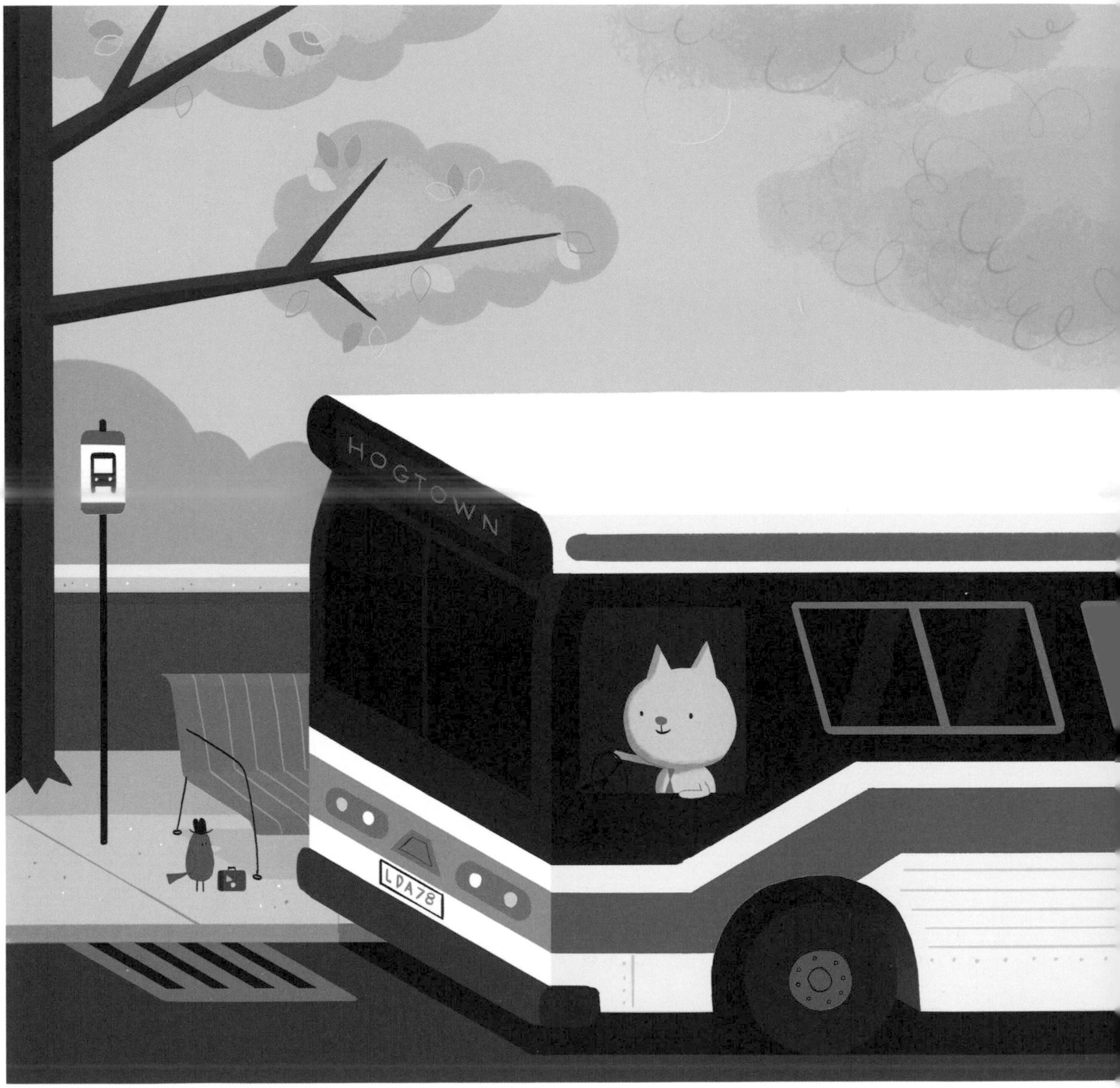
HOGTOWN
LDA78